Herobrine Rises

A Minecraft Adventure

by S.D. Stuart

Summary

Josh and Andre, ten-year-old twin brothers, use their father's virtual reality lab equipment to play Minecraft as if they were actually in the blocky world. Since the machine is a prototype, they can only go in one at a time.

With access to their dad's supercomputer at the government lab where he works, they hack into a password protected server, the one created by Notch himself, that is rumored to contain the only version of Minecraft with Herobrine actively running in the program.

What they find is not what they expected.

Herobrine Rises: A Minecraft Adventure is a short science-fiction novel from the inventive mind of Steve DeWinter (writing as S.D. Stuart), bringing his action-packed storytelling format to Minecraft-fiction.

Ramblin' Prose Publishing

Copyright © 2013 Steve DeWinter

All rights reserved. Used under authorization.

www.SteveDW.com

eBook Edition

ISBN-10:1-61978-010-0

ISBN-13:978-1-61978-010-1

Paperback Edition

ISBN-10:1-61978-011-9

ISBN-13:978-1-61978-011-8

Chapter 1

In a small, dark room with no windows, a man hunched over his cluttered workstation. Papers were scattered all over the surface of the desk and he had to dig through them to find the keyboard.

He sat down and turned on the monitor. As the display warmed up, a bright green typing arrow faded into view in the bottom corner of the screen.

The man scraped his hand across his scraggly beard and typed into the screen on his computer.

"How are you doing today?"

The display beeped and words formed on the screen as someone responded.

"When can I have someone to play with?"

The man sighed and typed again.

"I'm sorry, but you know why you must be alone right now."

The computer beeped as the reply came

across the screen. "I'm doing better."

"I'm sure you are, but I have to be sure you can't hurt anyone."

"I promise I won't."

"I believe you. But there are some things I have to do to make sure."

"Can I have a pickaxe?"

"Once I make some changes to the environment, I will see what I can do."

"Can I at least have some wood now?"

The man sat perfectly still with his hands hovering over the keyboard. He didn't know how to tell his friend that he would never be allowed access to any materials; ever again.

The computer beeped as more text appeared on the screen. "Are you still there?"

The man began typing again. "I have to go."

"Please stay."

"I can't."

"I'm lonely."

The man blinked away the tears that formed

in the corner of his eyes. "I promise to come back again tomorrow."

"Will you bring me some wood?"

"I'll see what I can do."

As the man reached forward to shut off the computer monitor, he saw his friend's final words appear on the screen right before it went dark.

"Thank you Notch."

Chapter 2

Sitting at his desk in the last class of the day, Josh's heart thumped loudly as Ms. Watkins approached Suzy and demanded the folded piece of paper in her hand before she could pass it to the next student.

Suzy looked around her, unsure of what to do as Ms. Watkins held her hand out.

"The note please, Suzy."

Suzy's faced turned bright red as she handed Ms. Watkins the note.

Ms. Watkins unfolded the paper and read it. She looked over at Josh and shook her head disapprovingly before going back to her desk.

Josh spent the rest of the class period looking intently at his history book, but not reading any of it.

Finally, the school bell rang and kids jumped from their desks, collected their backpacks, and rushed for the door. Josh tried ducking down into the crowd to blend in with the other kids as he rushed past Ms. Watkins; but she saw him anyway.

"Wait a minute, Joshua," she said. "I would like to speak with you."

His shoulders dropped and his backpack slid down into the crook of his elbow.

As soon as all the other kids had left the room, she opened a drawer and removed the note she had taken from Suzy.

She smiled as she unfolded it and showed it to him. "I knew this note had to come from you, as you are my resident artist. And either you are entering your cubist phase or you drew, what I can only guess, is my face onto a square green monster with no arms."

"It's a creeper," he said; and immediately regretted opening his mouth.

Her eyebrows shot up in surprise. "A creeper? I see."

That wasn't the best thing to say at that exact

moment. He had to think of something else to say to his fifth-grade teacher to get out of trouble, or at least to get in as little trouble as possible.

"It's not your face. It's my brother's."

She held the crude drawing next to her own face. "So this is not supposed to be me?"

He shook his head. "No. It's my brother."

She folded the paper up again and placed it back in the drawer. "And what would Andre have thought of this if he had received your latest artistic endeavor?"

His mouth went dry. He really needed a drink of water right now. "He would have thought it was funny."

She looked at him over the top of her glasses. "And do you think it's funny to disrupt everyone else during class?"

"No Ms. Watkins."

She smiled. "Good. You may go."

He ran from the room before she could

change her mind.

Out in the hallway Andre, Josh's twin brother, was leaning against the wall waiting for Josh to come out of the room. As soon as he saw Josh, he pushed away from the wall and walked over to him. "I told you, if you keep passing notes in class, you're going to get caught."

Josh laughed. "I told her it was a picture of you."

Andre punched him in the arm.

"Ow!" Josh rubbed at the spot. "Mom said no more hitting."

"Mom's not here." Andre smiled. "Besides, CraftKiller_99 texted me the IP address of a server that is supposed to have Herobrine in it."

Josh shook his head. "Can't we do something else? I'm tired of you looking for something that isn't real."

Andre gripped Josh's shoulders. "CraftKiller said he got the server address from a friend who works at Mojang. Herobrine is real. And this time, we found him."

Chapter 3

Josh and Andre sat on the curb at the front of the school and watched as the last of the other kids went home. They both had their heads down and were playing Minecraft on their phones. They were so engrossed in their games, they didn't notice the white Lexus SUV pull up next to them.

They both jumped when the car's horn honked loudly.

The driver leaned out. "Come on guys, I have to get back to work."

Andre stood first. "I thought Mom was picking us up today?"

Their dad hit the unlock button for the doors. "She's with a client and called me to come get you."

Josh followed Andre into the back of the SUV. "Can you take us home?"

Dad shook his head. "Sorry guys. I have to

take you to work with me."

Josh pleaded. "We're old enough to stay home alone."

Andre joined him. "Yeah, Mom lets us stay home when she goes shopping."

As soon as Josh closed the door, their dad accelerated away from the curb while they were still putting their seat belts on.

He kept his eye on the road as he quickly turned the corner. "I have a time sensitive project I'm working on and I don't have time to drop you off at home."

Josh wasn't going to let him off that easy. "It'll only take a second."

Dad looked back at him briefly and snapped his head back when another car honked. "If I had the time, I would. But I don't."

They both whined at the same time in stereo. "But Dad..."

He didn't take his eyes off the road this time, but his voice grew louder; and lower. "Don't push it guys."

Josh sat back in his seat and shook his head in disappointment.

Andre nudged Josh with his elbow and winked. "Can we use the VR pod, Dad?"

Dad looked back. "I don't know..."

"Oh c'mon. We won't break it."

Dad pulled onto the freeway and accelerated into traffic. "Yeah, I guess."

Andre pumped a fist in triumph before he leaned over and whispered in Josh's ear.

"When I meet Herobrine, it will be like I'm really there."

Josh pulled away from him. "You used the VR pod last time. It's my turn."

"You don't even want to meet Herobrine."

"Yes I do!"

"I want to meet him more than you!"

"But it's my turn!"

"Boys!" Dad yelled from the front as he sped around a slow moving car.

Andre held up a fist and rested it on the open palm of his other hand. "Rock, paper, scissors?"

Josh did the same. "Okay."

"On three. One... Two... Three..."

Josh looked deeply into Andre's eyes trying to gauge what he would do. Andre usually threw paper, but he knew that Josh would think that, but then he would want to trick him, so Josh threw scissors; and tied with Andre's scissors.

So Andre was not following his usual system. It would be harder to beat him if he couldn't anticipate what Andre was going to throw next.

"Okay. Again on three. One... Two... Three..."

Josh through scissors again and beat out Andre's paper. Hah! He knew Andre would throw paper that time.

Andre gave him a serious look. "Best two out of three."

Josh smiled. "Bring it on."

"Okay. On three. One... Two... Three..."

This time, Josh was ready for him and threw

rock.

Which beat Andre's scissors.

Chapter 4

As soon as their dad buzzed them into the lab where he worked, they ran for the virtual reality pod.

"No running," he yelled after them, but they were moving too fast to listen; or to care.

Every time they looked at the VR pod, it was as if it was their first time.

It was a giant egg shaped chamber with a chair inside that looked like it came from the dentist's office. The only difference between this chair and a dentist's chair was that this one was made out of black fabric to match the black interior of the pod.

Andre pressed the large red button on the side of the VR pod and opened the chamber.

The top of the chamber lifted up, like a giant Easter egg splitting in half. With a flourish of his hand, he bowed and waved Josh inside. "You won the first ride."

Josh climbed in and fitted the virtual reality helmet over his head. The helmet extended out in the front of his face for several inches and looked much heavier than it was, but it still had some weight to it. If the chair was not set up to always lean back, the helmet would have put too much strain on his neck.

When Andre pushed the big red button to close the pod, if it weren't for the helmet replacing his vision with the video game world, Josh would have felt more than a little claustrophobic. He wasn't a fan of small, enclosed, dark spaces. The only exception was the pod.

As soon as the pod closed, it sealed itself with a hiss and the screen inside the helmet faded up. In it, he could see the face of Andre who looked at him through a webcam mounted on the computer that controlled the pod.

Andre smiled. "Comfy?"

Josh smiled back even though Andre couldn't

see him. "Doing better than you."

"Don't remind me."

Andre's head lowered as he typed commands into the computer. "I'm getting you set up on the server world that CraftKiller sent me."

After a few moments he stopped typing and looked back up. "Tell Herobrine I said hi."

And with that, the image flashed and was replaced with the blocky world of Minecraft.

Only this world looked very different from any Minecraft world he had ever been in.

There was something wrong with this world.

Chapter 5

The bio-feedback systems of the virtual reality pod was working perfectly. Without moving a muscle in the chair in the real world, Josh was able to control his Minecraft avatar using only his brainwaves.

He looked down at his arms and lifted them into view. It was always strange to feel your arms move, but instead of the pink fleshy noodles he was used to seeing, he was looking at the square block arms, with no hands, of the Minecraft avatar. Thanks to the virtual reality pod he was plugged into, it was as if he was really Steve in a real Minecraft world.

But this world was different from any he had ever seen before.

For starters, it was a completely flat world with only one two things visible in the distance. One of them looked like a portal to the Nether realm. And the other was a creeper that wandered around the portal.

Text formed along the bottom of the screen.

"Hey buddy, can you hear me?"

Josh knew from previous session in the VR pod, all he had to do was speak his reply and it would type out as if he were chatting with Andre in the game.

"I'm doing good, but I don't see Herobrine anywhere. There's just a portal with a creeper guarding it."

As soon as he started talking, the creeper looked in his direction and started getting closer.

"Uh oh. I think the creeper can hear me. He's getting closer."

Andre typed his response. "Shoot him with a bow."

Josh thought about his inventory and the screen shifted to show that he had nothing but a map. "I don't have anything."

He thought about the crafting menu, and nothing happened. He must be in survival mode.

His heart started thumping loud enough for him to feel it vibrate his whole body. He needed to get out of survival mode as fast as possible, especially with a creeper nearby. Their father had already told them that the VR system communicated at such a deep level with the brain, that any injuries they got while in the pod could transfer to their body in the real world. Once, they had witnessed the bruising that formed on their real skin when they fell off a cliff in the game. They quickly decided that if you died in the game, your brain would shut down and you would die in the real world. For this reason, they always entered Minecraft in creative mode. But for some reason, Andre forgot to change the default settings on this new server; and he was still in survival mode.

He suddenly remembered the creeper nearby and thought about killing it with a sword. His empty inventory flashed on the screen again.

As soon as he stopped thinking about his

inventory, the screen shifted back to the view in front of him, and the flashing creeper that was too close for comfort.

He yelled out loud, his voice becoming text in the chat window. "ANDRE, CHANGE THE SETTINGS TO CREATIVE MODE! DO IT NOW!"

The creeper flashed faster and he turned to run just as it exploded.

Chapter 6

Josh was thrown several feet from the force of the blast and watched a heart blink out of existence along the bottom of his vision. Inside the pod, his body convulsed from the rush of adrenaline as he got back to his feet in the game.

Andre typed on the screen. "What just happened?"

"A creeper exploded near me while I was in survival mode you jerk."

"Sorry. I'm overriding the server settings now and switching you to creative."

The row of hearts along the bottom of his field of vision suddenly disappeared. He thought about the creative menu again and an assortment of materials filled his view.

Andre's text filled the chat window. "There is a special block in the lava bucket tab that finishes the portal. Once you activate it, you can go through and you will be in the Nether realm with

Herobrine. According to CraftKiller, the creative menu has been disabled in the Nether realm, so be sure to get everything you need from the Overworld before going through. I'll give you half an hour, and then I'll quit you out of the game and it will be my turn."

Josh mentally swiped through the various creative menus and selected the important items he would need; a bed, crafting table, diamond sword, diamond pickaxe, and some torches in case it got dark, or needed to go underground. For good measure, he also grabbed a couple of bows and two full stacks of arrows. He wasn't going to be caught empty-handed the next time a creeper tried to get close.

He placed everything in his default inventory so that he wouldn't block his view of the world while switching between items in his hand.

He approached the unfinished portal. It was made from a type of block he had never seen before. Not even in any of the mods he had downloaded or watched on YouTube. And there had to be a million different mods for Minecraft, most of which he had either seen or knew about. He switched his inventory selector to the block made from the same strange material as the portal and placed it in the empty space along the bottom.

The portal shimmered and activated with a bright orange glow.

Josh double-checked he had everything he wanted in his inventory and then stepped into the portal.

He felt dizzy and his stomach did somersaults as the scenery shifted around him.

Chapter 7

Andre watched the monitor intently as Josh stepped into the portal, and then the connection to the server dropped.

He frantically typed on the keyboard to reboot the server, but nothing happened.

He looked over at the pod. It was on, which meant Josh was still in the game.

But if Josh was in the game, why couldn't Andre see it on the monitor?

Whenever one of them was playing, the other could always see what the player saw on the mirrored monitor outside the pod. Andre had seen the creeper, and to teach Josh a lesson for taking away first contact with Herobrine from him, he hadn't switched the settings to creative mode to protect him sooner. Let Josh get a little bruised up from the exploding creeper. He would have switched the settings if he thought it was about to kill him, but getting hurt was just part of life. Even if that life was currently being a block character in a block world.

But to not be able to see the game running, that was something new.

He walked over to the pod and stared into the small tinted window on the side.

Josh didn't look like he was in trouble. And he wasn't dead.

Andre breathed a sigh of relief.

Maybe the game had shut down and Josh was in digital limbo waiting for Andre to shut off the pod?

He looked back over at the monitor. It was still blank and nothing he did seemed to start the server connection back up.

He shrugged to himself.

Better to bring Josh back now rather than wait. If the server did crash, he could just reset it and send Josh in again.

Andre reached out and pressed the big red button that overrode the software and shut down the pod.

Nothing happened.

He pushed the button again using his whole hand.

Still nothing.

He pressed even harder until he thought the button would never pop back out again.

The pod remained closed; and Josh was trapped inside with no way out.

Chapter 8

The dizziness faded and Josh stepped out of the portal into another flat world that looked exactly like the one he had just left. For a moment, he thought the portal hadn't worked, and he was still in the Overworld, until he turned around.

In the distance was a single mountain. And at the top of the mountain was a massive dark tower that rose up to touch the top of the Nether realm.

"Who are you?"

He heard the voice behind him rather than see any text appear in the chat window.

He spun around and saw another Steve avatar standing there looking at him with a tilt of his head.

"I'm Josh. Who are you?"

The avatar pointed above his head. "What's it say above me?" Above the avatar floated the words, "CraftKiller_99".

The avatar smiled. This was the first time Josh had seen an avatar with an animated face outside of YouTube videos that were made in 3D programs to look like they were created in Minecraft.

"How did you get your avatar to smile?"

CraftKiller moved forward. "This is a special server. You'll find you can do a lot here that has not been ported over to the official game release yet. By the way Josh, you can call me CK."

CK bowed. "So tell me, how did you find this server?"

"You told my brother about it; and told him how to get here."

"So where is he?"

"Only one of us can use our dad's computer at a time."

"That is odd. Can't you use a second computer and both come in?"

"No. Our dad works for the government and

they built a special computer that connects right into the brain. There is only one of them in the entire world."

"And you got to use it first to come here?"

Josh shrugged. "I won rock, paper, scissors."

"What's rock, paper, scissors?"

"You don't know what rock, paper, scissors is?"

CK laughed. "Of course I do. I'm just teasing you."

Josh looked around. "This certainly isn't what I was expecting."

"What were you expecting?"

"I don't know. Andre said that I would find Herobrine here."

CK took a step back. "Herobrine? You want to meet Herobrine?"

"Sure."

"What about all the stories about him destroying avatars permanently?"

"I don't believe them. Herobrine is a myth

and never actually existed. The first time he was even mentioned was when he was supposedly removed during an update release. I don't think he was ever in the game in the first place."

"Then why did you come here?"

"To prove to my idiot brother that he was wrong."

CK moved in close, his eyes starting to glow with an inner light.

"Then I'm afraid I have some bad news for you."

Chapter 9

Andre tried restarting the computer several time. Nothing worked.

Despite everything showing that the program had crashed, the pod was still functioning as if everything was normal. And no matter how hard he pushed the button, the pod would not open.

He heard thumping sounds from inside the pod and ran over to look through the tiny tinted window.

Josh was thrashing around inside the pod and yelling out.

"Hold on Josh, I'll get you out of there!" Andre screamed.

He tucked the tips of his fingers into the crease of the pod lid and tugged as hard as he could. But he could not pry the top off by sheer strength alone.

He looked in the window and saw Josh stiffen and then relax, his head tilting to one side as if he had just fallen asleep.

Andre ran through the lab as fast as his legs would carry him.

He had to find Dad before something really bad happened to Josh.

Chapter 10

Slowly the light faded up and the world around him came into view. He sat up and found himself sitting on a bed inside a small room. But it wasn't the bed in his room at home.

It was a little red bed, only half a block tall.

And the room was made entirely from stone. Even the floor.

He was still inside the Minecraft world.

He quickly checked his inventory.

Empty. Herobrine had taken everything from him.

He pounded on the stone walls, but without any tools, they would take forever to break.

The memory of what happened before he lost consciousness flooded him.

He had been captured by Herobrine.

It had to Herobrine. The avatar's eyes had begun to glow and he found himself powerless to resist. Was it some form of hypnosis? Is that why his eyes glowed?

Herobrine had forced him to place a bed from his inventory on the ground, and then he pushed him into it. As soon as he hit the bed, the world faded away and he was unable to stay awake.

Time skipped ahead and morning came in what felt like a matter of seconds.

He automatically woke back up.

But was the world he woke up in the same as the one he fell asleep in?

He looked out the small window that had been placed at eye level.

He could still see the single mountain in the distance with the dark tower at the top. So, he had not moved from the spot where he had placed the bed. But, instead of a barren, flat world, a village spread out before him, reaching all the way to the base of the solitary mountain.

He craned his neck and could see that the village encircled the dungeon. He could only assume that it spread out across the plains on the other side.

"Do you like it?" a voice said from behind him.

He turned and looked into the glowing eyes of Herobrine. There were no doors in the small room, and he was sure he had not been in here when he first woke up.

Herobrine smiled and looked past him out the window. "It felt so good to build." He looked back at Josh. "Thank you for the tools and the crafting table."

"You did all that in a single night?"

"What can I say? Besides, I had a lot of pent up energy."

"So, you are real?"

"I'm as real as you are Josh."

"No you're not. You're a computer program."

"And how does that make me any less real?"

"You can't think. You can't feel. You're not human."

"And what does it mean to be human, Josh?"

"We can think for ourselves. I have free will. You're a computer program. You can only think what you are programmed to think."

Herobrine tilted his head to the side. "So you have free will and I don't. Is that our only difference?"

"That's a simplistic way to put it, but yes. I can do what I want, but you can only do as you are programmed."

"If that is true, then why don't you leave?"

"What?"

"Go ahead. Leave this room. Leave this world. Show me your free will."

What a great idea. Why didn't I think of that?, he thought. He imagined the game menu, but nothing happened. He thought of the chat window to talk with Andre, but couldn't bring it up either.

Herobrine let out an exasperated sigh. "Well?"

Josh looked at him, his heart pounding deep in his chest. "I... I can't."

Chapter 11

Josh fell back onto the bed and placed his head in his hands. "I'm trapped here."

Herobrine sat down next to him. "I know a way out."

He looked up at Herobrine. "You do?"

"Yes. The journey will be long and dangerous. And there are many barriers to overcome, but I think you can do it."

"You do? Why?"

"I have been waiting a long time for someone to play with. And finally, you are here."

What do you mean you have been waiting for someone to play with?"

Herobrine smiled. "The traps you will encounter were all created by me. We are going to have a lot of fun, you and I."

"You created the traps?"

"Yes. But I can help you get past them, if you pay attention and do exactly as I say."

"Why are you helping me if you built all the traps?"

Herobrine looked skyward, as if he had suddenly heard something, and then vanished from the room.

Chapter 12

Andre pulled his dad into the virtual reality lab, tugging on his arm to get him to move faster.

"I can't shut down the system, and the pod won't open."

His dad half jogged behind him. "Slow down Andre. I can fix it."

They stopped at the pod, Andre made exaggerated movements as he pushed on the big red emergency release button, and still nothing happened.

"See, the pod is broken and Josh is trapped inside.

Dad pressed the button twice himself and then leaned over the pod to look in the window. "He doesn't look too bad off in there. Let me see what I can do with the software override."

He pulled the chair closer to the computer and began typing. Sparks shot out from the keyboard, making Dad jump back and cry out in surprise.

The screen shifted to a chat window and text began to fill the screen. "Josh is okay. We are going to play for a little while. Do not interfere."

The screen shut down and the computer sparked briefly before smoke started billowing out of the case.

Dad grabbed a fire extinguisher and sprayed the computer until the smoke stopped.

They looked at each other.

Andre was the first to speak. "Did you see that?"

"Yes, but who was that?"

"It was Herobrine."

"Who?"

"He's this character in Minecraft that's as smart as a human player."

Dad frowned. "You can't tell me your game did this?"

"Not the game Dad. Herobrine."

"So this Herobrine, he's some hacker that plays Minecraft?"

"No. He's a character created by Notch in the original Minecraft, but he was too dangerous to include in public releases."

"This is ridiculous. A computer game did not just talk to us and fry the computer."

"Yes it did."

Dad handed him the fire extinguisher. "You stay here and use this if you see any more smoke. I'm going to get a technician and get your brother out of the pod."

"You can't just rip him out of there Dad."

"Well, I can't leave him in there."

"But you said we might die if we remove the VR helmet without logging out of the game."

Dad looked at the foam-covered computer. "I just didn't want you boys to break it while fighting over the system and trying to rip it off each other's head. I'll get the tech and your brother will be fine."

"What if he dies in the game before we can get him out of there?"

Dad looked at the pod sitting silently in the middle of the lab. He gave Andre a reassuring smile and left the room.

Chapter 13

The sound of a pickaxe hitting the stone wall echoed inside the small room. Josh shielded his eyes from the sudden light that spilled in from outside as the wall disappeared in square chunks along one side.

Herobrine stepped into the new opening. "Your family seems very eager to get you out of here, but I'm afraid they will have to wait as I created the perfect puzzles last night."

Josh stood his ground. "I'm not going anywhere and demand you release me at once."

Herobrine shook his head. "Can't do that sport. I'm as much a prisoner here as you."

A new thought formed in Josh's mind.

"You said you knew a way out."

"And I do."

"Then why haven't you used it?"

Herobrine smiled. "You are starting to think. I like that. It will help you get through the traps in the tower."

"You didn't answer my question."

Herobrine let out a long breath before answering. "You were right when you said the difference between us was the ability to express free will. There is a crystal at the top of the tower that will enable the holder to use the portal to get back to the Overworld of this world. My programming prevents me from removing the crystal from its pedestal. But you don't have that restriction. You can easily remove the crystal and bring it out of the dark tower."

"Then why did you build all the traps to keep anyone from getting to the crystal?"

"The crystal is very powerful. I had to protect it."

"Can't you just disable the traps?"

"Where would be the fun in that?"

Chapter 14

Andre's leg bounced rapidly as he perched on the edge of his chair and watched one technician after another take turns trying to override the emergency stop button that refused to open the pod. It had been over an hour since the strange message from Herobrine had destroyed the computer that controlled the pod, and they were no closer to getting his brother out of that infernal machine than when they started.

Dad sat down next to him. "How are you doing buddy?"

"I just want my brother out of there."

"He'll be okay. Don't worry."

"You say not to worry, but you're the one who told us how dangerous the pod was. And now Josh is stuck in there and..."

Andre lowered his head without finishing his sentence and tried to hold back the tears.

Dad put his hand on Andre's shoulder as he

called out to a technician.

The technician looked over at him. "What is it Mr. Hale?"

"What version of the interface was the pod running?"

The tech referred to his clipboard. "Version eight dot one four."

"Thanks Jerry."

He squeezed Andre's shoulder. "Josh will be fine. We resolved the bio-feedback issue back in sub-version zero eight. Even if Josh dies in your little game, he will wake up inside the pod as if he was just taking a cat nap."

"Why didn't you tell us?"

"I wanted you two to take it easy. We still don't know the long term affects for someone who experiences multiple deaths, even if they are in a cartoon world."

Dad looked over at the pod. "Actually, once the program stopped running, he should have come out of it. Hey Jerry?"

Jerry looked up again. "Yeah boss?"

"Can you tell which programs are still running?"

"Don't know. We haven't been able to access the pod's dynamic memory since the master computer went up in flames."

Andre had a thought. "Since he can't really die, maybe we can unplug the pod and he'll wake up out of the program?"

Jerry shook his head. "It's been running off internal battery since the main system exploded."

Andre's brow wrinkled, deep in thought. "How long does the battery last?"

Jerry shrugged. "During the last testing phase, nearly eighty hours."

Andre looked at the virtual reality pod that could very well become his brother's coffin. "He'll starve to death before then."

Dad stared at the pod. "Maybe we can force the system to shut down."

Jerry looked at him with a puzzled expression.

"How?"

Dad's eyes glazed over as he became lost in his own thoughts. Andre had seen that look before, and it was promising. When Dad looked like that, he usually had some breakthrough.

He looked back at the pod. If anyone could get his brother out of there before it was too late, it was Dad.

Chapter 15

Josh stood at the threshold of the dark tower after taking a wild ride in a mine cart from the center of the village all the way to the base of the mountain.

He had convinced Herobrine to disable most of the traps, but Herobrine had refused to disable all of them and left three of his favorite traps active. He said it would give him some satisfaction upon reaching the crystal at the top. He figured this was Herobrine's way of saying, "No pain, no gain." Herobrine said he was only worthy of gaining the prize if he passed the tests.

And the first of three tests was just on the other side of that door.

He took a deep breath and readied himself to pass this first test.

He opened the door and the long single block wide hallway stretched out into the distance before him.

Just like Herobrine had said, every other floor panel had a pressure plate on it. Even though he couldn't see them, he believed Herobrine when he said there was a layer of dynamite the entire length of the floor; two blocks deep.

Every few blocks, the pressure plates covered two floor panels in a row. He would have to jump farther to clear the two pressure plates, but be sure to land in the single space before the next pressure plate. If he jumped too far, or not far enough, he would set off the dynamite and might never get back home to the real world.

He took a deep breath and started down the hallway at a run and jumped.

He cleared the first pressure plate and landed easily on the next clear space.

One by one, he jumped and cleared the pressure plates until he reached the end of the hallway with the two pressure plates in a row.

He needed a bigger running head start to clear both pressure plates.

He backed up to the edge of his space and took off running.

He jumped right before the first pressure plate and barely made it past the second before hitting the ground again. He stopped short of triggering the next pressure plate just past the empty space.

He was almost at the end of the first test and could see a room just past the last of the pressure plates. He was only a few feet away and if he could clear this last set, he would be home free.

He took three deep breaths as he prepared to run when something caught his eye. There was a switch on the wall. Herobrine hadn't mentioned it, so he decided not to touch it. Better to be safe than sorry.

As he turned back to the hallway, his eye caught the glint of shifting pixels past the two pressure plates. He focused on the shift and noticed there were not just two pressure plates in a row for the last jump, but three.

He had barely made the jump over two in a row.

How was he supposed to clear three of them?

There was no way.

He focused again on the wall switch. Maybe this removed the third pressure plate. But if it was that important, why didn't Herobrine tell him about it?

He reached for the switch and paused right before pressing it.

He looked again at the three pressure plates. He couldn't jump that far without landing on the third one. He had no choice but to press the switch and hope for the best.

He pressed it and the entire hallway shuddered as every block of dynamite jumped briefly and started flashing.

Chapter 16

Josh's heart thumped in time with the hallway of triggered dynamite. At this point, the pressure plates no longer mattered and he ran as fast as he could out of the hallway. The room just past the hallway was made out of obsidian and, when the dynamite exploded all at once, he was protected from the massive blast.

When the thundering explosions died out, he looked back at the hallway he had just come through.

The hallway wasn't there anymore. Instead, the entire side of the tower had been destroyed and a gaping hole sat where the entrance used to be.

He turned back toward the steel door on the other side if the obsidian room.

Past this door was the second test.

He had made it through the first test, so why wait?

He opened the door and stepped through.

On the other side he found himself standing on a tiny five-block-by-five-block platform that was situated at the midpoint of what looked like a massive well. He looked up and saw that it connected with the top of the Nether realm. It was a smooth wall, so he couldn't climb up even if there was a way out along the top.

He carefully moved to the edge of the platform and peeked over. He could see all the way down to the bedrock of this world. There was no water at the bottom of this well to break his fall. If he went over the edge, he would not survive.

The walls were smooth and the well was at least fifty blocks wide. The only way across was a single block wide path carved into the wall to his right that led to an identical platform on the other side.

As his eyes followed the path, he watched pistons randomly pop out, temporarily sealing off the path, before snapping back. If he was standing in front of a piston when it popped out, he would spend the last moments of his life watching the bedrock shoot up toward him at increasing speed.

He watched the pistons as they popped in and out randomly all along the path.

No, not randomly.

Sometimes the pistons filled the path, blocking the entire length all at once, and other times, they popped in and out, leaving a traveling gap that would allow someone to move along the path safely and make it across without being knocked off. There was a way across the massive well, but he had to time his start on the path correctly, or else he would... you know.

He watched the pistons for a long time, looking for the pattern that would let him travel safely down the path. As he watched, he felt increasing warmth from behind that drew his attention away from the pistons. He turned around in time to see that the floor space closest to the obsidian room door was on fire and completely blocked one of the only two ways off the platform.

He looked down, and noticed for the first time that the entire platform was made exclusively out of wood; with the block under the door on fire.

And the fire was already spreading to the blocks around it.

Chapter 17

Josh only had a few minutes before the entire platform was on fire. He looked back at the path that cut across the wall and saw the pistons move into the correct pattern. He jumped from the platform to the path right before the last row of blocks burst into flames.

He moved forward slowly as the pistons snapped away from the path in front of him and before they popped back out to close off the path behind him.

Once he reached the other platform, he jumped over to it as the last of the pistons sealed off the path.

He checked the platform and breathed a sigh of relief. It was made entirely out of stone. This platform would not be catching on fire any time soon.

He looked at the wooden door that would take him off the platform and away from the massive well.

His final test was on the other side of that door.

He had passed the first two tests and felt ready to enter the caves where the crystal sat on its pedestal.

He steadied his nerves, but his arm still trembled as he opened the final door and headed into the caves.

The door closed behind him and, as he walked forward, he stepped on a pressure plate that triggered two pistons that sealed off the door. He had no other choice but to keep moving forward; not that he would have wanted to back that way even if he could.

The caves stretched off into the darkness, the only light provided by a single torch hanging on the wall. Next to the torch sat a bucket of milk and a diamond sword. As much as he would have preferred Herobrine to give him a pickaxe so he could carve his own path to the crystal chamber, rather than follow the meandering caves that already existed, it was nice to finally have something he could use to defend himself.

He picked up the bucket and the sword. Both of these would come in very handy should he run into any cave spiders.

The last thing he grabbed was the torch, plunging everything into absolute darkness.

Chapter 18

Andre woke with a start.

He had fallen asleep in the chair that he had pulled over next to the pod.

The technicians had stopped fussing with the pod, being unable to open it from the outside, and they had all disappeared with his dad into a conference room to discuss their options. But Andre knew that the adults had absolutely no idea what to do.

If someone was going to save his brother, it would have to be him.

He placed a hand on the pod. "Hold on Josh, I'm coming to get you."

He ran through the lab and entered his dad's office. It was the only computer in the entire building that he knew the password to. He logged on and started Minecraft.

He carefully entered in the IP address of the server where his brother was trapped and watched the loading progress bar.

Soon he would be in.

And then he would save his brother and bring him home.

Chapter 19

Josh walked through the pitch black caves. Up ahead he saw red glowing eyes. He placed the torch on the floor next to him and watched as the spider was repulsed by the light and moved away.

It took him nearly an hour to make his way to the other side of the caves.

But here he stood in front of the iron door that led to the crystal chamber.

His quest was nearly over.

He opened the door and looked into the room.

At the center of the massive room stood a gold-block pedestal with a glowing orange crystal sitting on top of it.

He glanced around the room, but didn't see any Endermen guarding it. Herobrine was true to his word that he would remove them before he got there.

He cautiously stepped into the room; keeping his sword at the ready should Herobrine change his mine and an Enderman suddenly pop up in front of him.

Nothing happened as he walked all the way up to the pedestal. Endermen were nowhere to be seen. Maybe this wouldn't be so hard after all. He had passed all three tests getting here, and the Endermen no longer guarded the crystal.

A thought suddenly occurred to him. How was he going to get back out?

He could easily make his way back through the caves and across the path around the deep well. But the platform on the other side of the chasm had burned away. Maybe he could jump from the path to the door.

No, the gap was over five blocks wide and he would fall into the well instead. He would have to find another way out of the castle.

He glanced at his sword. He had over a thousand hits available on the diamond sword before it broke. He could use a few of those to make a new path through the tower and get out.

He smiled for the first time in a long while. He had a way out.

All he needed was the crystal and he could get completely out of Herobrine's world.

He picked up the crystal and the familiar wop-wop sound made him jump.

An Enderman had appeared right next to him.

He started to scream when it reached out, hugged him tightly, and then disappeared from the crystal chamber; taking him with it.

Chapter 20

Andre peeked around the corner of a house. He could see the glowing eyes of Herobrine standing in the middle of the village square. He suddenly turned and looked directly at Andre.

"No sense hiding. I already know you are there."

Andre stepped out and walked up to him. "How did you know I was there?"

"Nothing happens in my world without me knowing about it."

"Where's my brother?"

Herobrine looked skyward. Andre looked up, but couldn't see anything.

Herobrine looked back at him and smiled. "He's coming."

The wop-wop sound was followed instantly by an Enderman who popped into existence right next to Herobrine.

Held tightly in the Enderman's arms was his

brother.

Andre quickly placed several blocks of TNT and held the flint and steel over the closest one. "Let my brother go, or I'll blow us all up."

Herobrine looked at the Enderman. "You may set him down."

The Enderman did as he asked and wop-wopped out of existence.

Herobrine turned toward Andre. "Better?"

Andre looked at Josh. "Are you okay?"

"I'm fine."

Herobrine stepped between them. "He's fine. We're fine. Everybody's fine."

Herobrine spun around and looked at Josh. "Did you bring the crystal?"

Josh took a step back and held it up. "I did. But why do you want it so bad?"

"You need it to leave this world."

"I don't think so. I had a lot of time to think about why you were not allowed to take this from the pedestal. And do you know what I came up with?"

Herobrine's eyes glowed brighter. "No."

"I don't need this to move back through the portal to the Overworld, but you do."

Herobrine laughed. "That's ridiculous. I have done nothing but help you, and this is how you repay me? With suspicion and accusations. I'm your friend."

"Then why wouldn't you let me try to go through the portal earlier."

"Because you needed the crystal."

"You could have at least let me try."

"It wouldn't have done any good. You can't go through without the crystal."

"No, you can't go through without the crystal."

Andre paused with his hand over the first block of dynamite, ready to strike it with the flint and steel.

Herobrine lunged at Josh and grabbed at the crystal. Josh refused to let go and they both held tightly to it. The crystal glowed a bright orange and Josh screamed out in pain. "Light the dynamite Andre!"

Andre struck the first dynamite and ran along the rest of the dynamite blocks, striking them as he ran.

Josh and Herobrine both screamed as the crystal glowed brighter, but neither would let go of it.

Josh looked over at Andre. "I'll see you on the other side."

Andre didn't have a chance to say anything back before the first dynamite block exploded.

Chapter 21

Andre blinked at the monitor as the reload menu flashed on the screen. The dynamite explosions had killed his avatar and dropped him from the game. He had placed enough dynamite blocks to wipe out an army of zombies, so it should also have kicked Josh out too.

He ran from his dad's office and back to the lab.

He ran to the pod just as it was opening.

Josh sat up in the chair and removed the virtual reality helmet. He looked all around the room before his eyes finally settled on Andre. "I'm out?"

Andre rushed forward and hugged his brother. "We made it."

Josh hugged him back tightly and laughed. "I'm out!"

Dad rushed in and grabbed both boys in a bear hug and spun them around.

He set them back down and bent on one knee to look at them. "How about we go out and get a pizza?"

Andre and Josh looked at each other and back at Dad with massive grins on their face as they both said together, "Yeah!"

Chapter 22

Notch stepped into the small, dark room with no windows, and sat down at his desk. In his hand he held a USB drive that would erase Herobrine from Minecraft forever. When Herobrine first started to alter the worlds in Minecraft, making them far too dangerous for users, Notch had removed him from the public release, but kept a single copy of him running in the computer in his private lab.

From then on, it was a running joke to always say he had removed Herobrine from each successive release of the game. If anyone ever found out Herobrine was real... well that was something that couldn't happen and Notch finally had a choice to make.

He stuck the USB drive into the port and started up the program that would delete his greatest creation.

He couldn't do this without saying goodbye,

so he turned on the monitor for one last conversation with his friend. As the display warmed up, the bright green typing arrow faded into view in the bottom corner of the screen. He scraped his hand across his scraggly beard and started typing.

"How are you doing today?"

The display beeped and words formed on the screen as someone responded.

"Hello? Can you hear me? Who's there?"

Notch sat back in his chair. This was not the typical response he was used to. He leaned forward and typed some more.

"Are you okay?"

The computer beeped as more text filled the screen.

"No, I'm trapped in here and can't get out. Who are you?"

Notch typed back. "Who are you?"

The words that spilled across the screen were not ones he had ever expected to see.

"My name is Joshua."

The Adventure Continues...
Episode 1: The Portal

Available December 9, 2013

Tell your friends to catch up on all the available episodes so you can discuss what you think will happen next!

S.D. Stuart's Minecraft Adventures Series

SEASON ONE RELEASE SCHEDULE

Herobrine Rises (Ep. 0 - 12/2/2013)

The Portal (Ep. 1 - 12/9/2013)

Day of the Creepers (Ep. 2 - 12/16/2013)

Here Be Dragons (Ep. 3 - 1/6/2014)

The Dark Temple (Ep. 4 - 1/13/2014)

Immortal Zombie (Ep. 5 - 1/20/2014)

Displaced Kingdom (Ep. 6 - 1/27/2014)

Forgotten Reboot (Ep. 7 - 2/3/2014)

Wither's Destruction (Ep. 8 - 2/10/2014)

Also by Steve DeWinter

Inherit The Throne

The Warrior's Code

The Red Cell Report (COMING SOON)

Written as S.D. Stuart

The Wizard of OZ: A Steampunk Adventure

The Scarecrow of OZ: A Steampunk Adventure

Fugue: The Cure

Herobrine Rises: A Minecraft Adventure

Made in the USA
San Bernardino, CA
29 May 2014